BOOKS BY MARCIA BROWN

THE LITTLE CAROUSEL

STONE SOUP

HENRY-FISHERMAN

DICK WHITTINGTON AND HIS CAT

SKIPPER JOHN'S COOK

PUSS IN BOOTS

THE STEADFAST TIN SOLDIER

CINDERELLA [*Caldecott Medal*]

THE FLYING CARPET

FELICE

by Marcia Brown

CHARLES SCRIBNER'S SONS, NEW YORK

Printed in the United States of America

LIBRARY OF CONGRESS CATALOG CARD NUMBER 58-11640

E-12.66(AJ)

TO HELEN,

who heard *Ecco!* in the night with me.

FELICE

In Venice

the sky is full of pigeons, the canals are full of gondolas, and the streets are full of cats.

Some cats wear red ribbons and eat fresh sardines and liver from plates. Other cats wear no ribbons and eat spaghetti from newspapers. And still others are lucky if they get a crust of bread or an old fish head.

> Fuffi, Micetta, Tito and Fifi
> Popo, Miciú, Tuffi and Mimi—

But there was one little striped cat that had no name because he had no one to call him. He had to hunt for his food because he had no one to feed him. He had no home at all.

Every day when old Lotta brought a paper of spaghetti, the big cats, the tough cats with fringed ears, all came running. But the little striped cat was afraid to go near when the big cats came.

The little cat crossed the square and smelled around the stand where Anna was selling her scarves and beads. But Anna was too busy to pay attention to him.

He went over to where Giovanni was unloading his barca of flowers for the hotels on the Grand Canal. But Giovanni didn't even see the small striped cat under the spotted leaf.

Hopefully he padded after Salvatore the postman, who was dropping the mail into the baskets that people let down from the high balconies. But there was nothing for him—nothing at all.

Everybody knew him—the little cat that was always alone.

And Gino the boy knew him—but the little striped cat didn't know that. He was too busy fishing in the canal for scraps of garbage among the paper boats.

But if Venice is a city of cats, it is most of all a city of canals—where people ride in long slim boats called gondolas. Gino was learning to be a gondolier like his father Marco. In the early morning the Grand Canal swarmed with gondolas and barcas loaded with fruits for the market, wine, flowers, coal and furniture.

Learning to be a gondolier was exciting enough. But what Gino wanted most in the world was a cat, just like

the little cat he saw fishing. "A little cat could ride in the gondola with us . . ." he said to his father. But just then a load of melons crossed in front of them, and a *vaporetto* whisked by in a wash of waves. Gino had no time then to think of cats.

But he didn't forget the little striped cat.

That afternoon in the siesta hour when the gondolas slept like sleepy swans and the whole city took a breath after its lunch, the little cat strolled down the street. Suddenly, he heard a soft whistle, and—*Ecco!* A basket dropped down in front of him and in the basket—his dinner!

And then came the *festa* with its fireworks and lanterns on the canal. Gino listened hard for the little cat's serenade among the other songs of the night. But that night the little cat had stolen a ride in a gondola just to see how it felt.

And every night after that, when Marco's gondola had nosed its way into the landing stage, the little cat would wait below Gino's window until—*Ecco!* the light would appear and down would come the basket with his supper.

But fish were hard for other cats to catch.

One night after the fast evening games were over and the children had gone home, the street was quiet. A big black cat saw the basket come down. He crept up behind the little striped cat.

Swish fanned the tails and W-a-a-a-a-a-a-a-a-a-ah rose the wails.

Then—in a flash—

Pffffffffffffffft!

The black cat was a seasoned fighter. Splash! The little striped cat found himself in the canal!

But Gino heard the splash and—

Ecco! Baskets can be used for more things than two!

Marco covered the gondola for the night and came into the house. He looked at the little wet cat. Then he looked at Gino.

"With all the cats in Venice, you choose *this* one?"

Gino looked at his father. "Could we call him Felice?"

Marco nodded and smiled. "And now the basket will be used for mail again, eh Gino?"

The next night
Marco's gondola
slipped silently
through the still waters
of the canal. The only
sounds were a footfall
in the night, the
dripping oars and a
far-off song.

Suddenly a light
bloomed around a
corner. Marco nodded
to Gino.

"Ohe!" The boy's
clear voice rang out
in the night, as if
to say, "Wait, ahead
there! Here we come,
my father,
Felice and I!"

For now
the little cat
had a home and he
had a name.
FELICE!